This Boxer Books paperback belongs to

. . . .

www.boxerbooks.com

The Fox and the Hen

Eric Battut

Boxer Books

One morning Henrietta Hen laid her very first egg.

"I wonder what this is," she said to herself.

Then along came Red Fox.

"What a nice egg!" he said.
"Would you like to swap it for this tasty, juicy worm?"

"Oh, yes please," said Henrietta Hen,
and she gave her egg to Red Fox.

When the other animals on the farm heard what Henrietta had done, they couldn't believe their ears!

"Oh, Henrietta," said Goose, "your egg is precious. You need to look after it and keep it warm. Red Fox will eat it!"

Henrietta Hen felt very sad. She should never have given away her beautiful egg.

"Don't worry," said Cow. "We'll find a way to get it back."

So Henrietta Hen and Rabbit went to see Red Fox.

"Red Fox," said Henrietta Hen, "would you like to swap that egg for these seeds from Rabbit's garden? They will grow into beautiful, colourful vegetables."

"No, thank you," said Red Fox. "I don't have a garden. And anyway, I'd much rather have a hard-boiled egg for my breakfast."

So Henrietta Hen tried again. This time, Goose came along.

"Red Fox," she said, "would you like to swap that egg
for some beautiful white feathers from Goose?
They will make a soft and fluffy pillow for your bed.
What do you say?"

"No need," said Red Fox. "My bed is already nice and soft.
Besides, I'd rather have a soft poached egg."

Henrietta Hen went away and thought hard.
Then she went back to Red Fox with Goat.

"Red Fox," she said, "would you like to exchange that
egg for this delicious cheese from Goat? It's soft and
creamy and oh so yummy!"

"Absolutely not," said Red Fox. "I already have plenty
of cheese. And anyway, I'm in the mood for an omelette."

But Henrietta didn't give up. Back she went with Sheep.

"Red Fox," she said, "would you like to swap that egg
for this beautiful wool from Sheep? It will make
a cosy jumper to keep you warm in winter."

"Out of the question," said Red Fox. "I already have
a furry red coat to keep me warm. Besides, I'd prefer
a scrambled egg."

So Henrietta tried again. Pig came with her.

"Red Fox," said Henrietta Hen, "would you like to swap
that egg for this nice jar of marmalade that Pig has made?"

"Oh, no," said Red Fox. "I can't stand marmalade.
I'd much rather have a delicious fried egg for breakfast."

But still Henrietta Hen did not give up. She and Cow went back to see Red Fox one more time.

"Red Fox," she said, "would you like to swap that egg for some delicious, creamy milk from Cow?"

"No way," said Red Fox. "I don't want any milk. I'm going to have a lovely soft-boiled egg instead."

Henrietta Hen didn't know what to do! How would she get her beautiful egg back? All the animals thought very, very hard.

Suddenly Henrietta Hen had an idea. "We need to find an egg even bigger and more beautiful than mine!" she said. "Red Fox will never be able to refuse that."

The animals looked all over the farm until they found an enormous stone. Then they painted it carefully with some white paint. It really did look like a gigantic egg!

Then Henrietta Hen ran straight back to Red Fox.

"Look what I found!" she said, showing Red Fox
the giant egg. "Would you like to swap that
teeny tiny egg for this great big one?"

"Oh, yes!" said Red Fox, licking his lips.

So Henrietta picked up her very small, very precious egg,
and carried it carefully home.

When Henrietta got back to the farm, her egg began to wobble and wiggle and shake, and a little yellow chick stuck its head out of the top.

Henrietta was the happiest hen in the world.

And what about Red Fox?

Well, he quickly built a fire, put the giant egg in a giant pot and waited impatiently to enjoy his giant hard-boiled egg.

But that giant egg turned out to be a whole lot harder than Red Fox expected.

THE END

First published in hardback in Great Britain in 2010 by Boxer Books Limited.
First published in paperback in Great Britain in 2015 by Boxer Books Limited.
www.boxerbooks.com

Text and illustrations copyright © 2008 Eric Battut
Original French edition copyright © 2008 Editions Milan – 300, rue Léon Joulin – 31101 Toulouse Cedex 9 – France
Boxer® Books is a registered trademark of Boxer Books Limited.

English translation copyright © 2010 Boxer Books Limited

The illustrations were prepared using acrylic paints.
The text is set in Adobe Garamond Pro.

ISBN 978-1-907152-84-9

1 3 5 7 9 10 8 6 4 2

Printed in Malaysia

All of our papers are sourced from managed forests and renewable resources.

Boxer® Books
The Art of Storytelling™
Celebrating 10 years

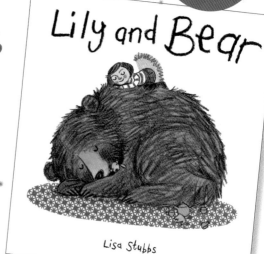

Lily and Bear

Lisa Stubbs

with a new classic, *Lily and Bear* by Lisa Stubbs.
Plus a stunning array of superb picture books and
board books from Laura Ellen Anderson, Tad Hills,
Algy Craig Hall, Britta Teckentrup and Jonathan Allen
. . . *and that's just for starters!*

www.boxerbooks.com